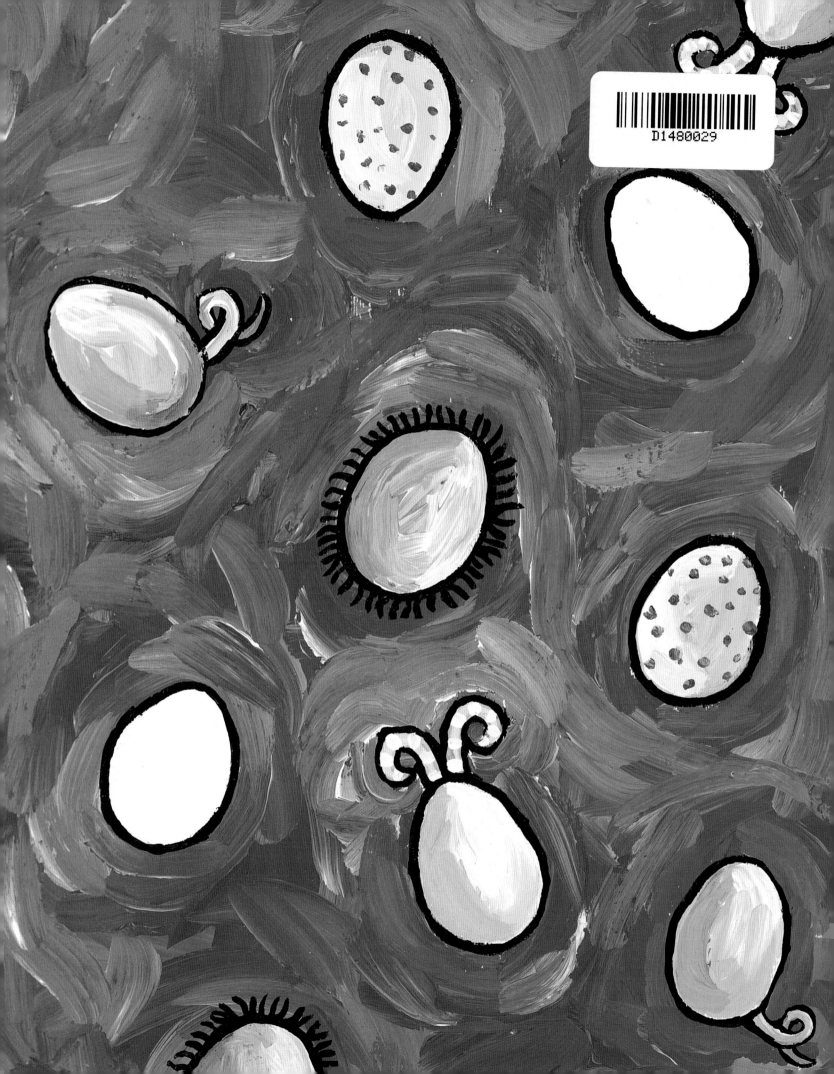

For my little, big sister
Joyce Dunbar

**For all factory farm animals,
that one day they will be as free
as the animals in Eggday.**
Jane Cabrera

Sandy Creek
NEW YORK

An Imprint of Sterling Publishing
387 Park Avenue South
New York, NY 10016

SANDY CREEK and the distinctive Sandy Creek logo are registered
trademarks of Barnes and Noble, Inc.

First published in 1999 by David and Charles Children's Books
Published in this edition in 2007 by Gullane Children's Books

Text © 1999 by Joyce Dunbar
Illustrations © 1999 by Jane Cabrera

This 2013 edition published by Sandy Creek.

ISBN 978-1-4351-4575-7

Printed and bound in Heshan, China
Lot #:
10 9 8 7 6 5 4 3 2 1
10/12

Eggday

Joyce Dunbar

Pictures by
Jane Cabrera

Sandy Creek
NEW YORK

Dora, the duck, said to Pogson, the pig, "Tomorrow is **Eggday**."

"What's **Eggday**?" asked Pogson.

"We are having a **best egg competition**," said Dora.

"But what can I bring?" asked Pogson.
"A **pig egg**," said Dora,
and she waddled over to tell Humphrey, the horse.

"Tomorrow is **Eggday**," said Dora.
"What's **Eggday**?" asked Humphrey.
"We are having a **best egg competition**," said Dora.
"But what can I bring?" said Humphrey.
"A **horse egg**," said Dora,
and she waddled over to tell Gideon, the goat.

"Tomorrow is **Eggday**," said Dora.

"What's **Eggday**?" asked Gideon.

"We are having a **best egg competition**," said Dora.

"But what can I bring?" asked Gideon.

"A **goat egg**," said Dora,

and she waddled back to her nest.

"Where will I get a **pig egg**?"
Pogson, the pig, asked
Humphrey, the horse.

"Where will I get a **horse egg**?"
Humphrey, the horse, asked Gideon, the goat.

"Where will I get a **goat egg**?"
Gideon, the goat, asked himself.

Hetty Hen came to see what the matter was.
"What's all the fuss?" she asked.

"It's **Eggday** tomorrow," said Pogson,
"I am trying to lay a **pig egg**."
"But pigs don't lay eggs," said Hetty.
"Pigs have piglets. And you're not even a sow."

"And I am trying to lay
a **horse egg**," said Humphrey.
"But horses don't lay eggs," said Hetty.
"Horses have foals.
And you're not even a mare."

"And I am trying to lay a **goat egg**," said Gideon.

"But goats don't lay eggs," said Hetty.

"Goats have kids. And you're a billy goat, not a nanny goat."

"But Dora says it's **Eggday** tomorrow," said Pogson.

"**What's Eggday?**" asked Hetty.

"We are having a **best egg competition**,"
said Pogson, "and we all have to take an egg."
"Wait here a moment," said Hetty,
"and I'll see what I can find in my coop."

Hetty came back with three eggs.
"Here's one for you," she said to Pogson.
"Give it a short curly tail, and it will look like a **pig egg**."
"Here's one for you, Humphrey," said Hetty.
"Give it a hairy brown mane, and it will look like a **horse egg**."
"What about me?" said Gideon.
"Here's one for you, Gideon. Give it a curved pair of horns,
and it will look like a **goat egg**," said Hetty.

So they all went away with their eggs.

In the morning, they met up again. Hetty was last to arrive. "**Happy Eggday!**" they said to one another, proudly showing off their eggs.

Hetty seemed the proudest of all as she
showed them a beautiful, smooth, speckled egg.
"I laid this especially!" she clucked.
"Where's Dora?"

"Let's go and find Dora," said Humphrey, and they went along to the hayloft where Dora had made her nest. "Dora! Dora!" called Pogson. **"It's Eggday today!** Come and see my **pig egg**. My pig egg has a short curly tail."

"And my **horse egg** has a hairy brown mane!" called Humphrey.
"And my **goat egg** has a curved pair of horns!" called Gideon.
"And my **hen egg** is smooth
with brown speckles!" called Hetty.

There was silence for a while,
then Dora started to quack.
"I've changed my mind," said Dora.
"It isn't **Eggday** anymore."
"Well, what day is it?"
asked Pogson.

"It's DUCKLING DAY!"

Dora quacked proudly.
And she lifted up her wing so that the animals could peep underneath.

Well—you can guess who had the best duckling!